This book belongs to:

_____

_____

_____

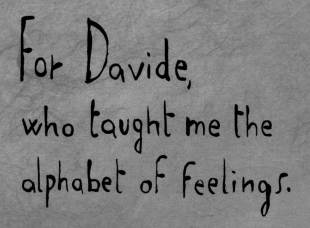

For Davide,
who taught me the
alphabet of feelings.

This edition published by Parragon in 2013
Parragon
Chartist House
15-17 Trim Street
Bath BA1 1HA, UK
www.parragon.com

Published by arrangement with Meadowside Children's Books
185 Fleet Street, London, EC4A 2HS

Text and illustrations © Eva Montanari 2010

ISBN 978-1-4723-1115-3

Printed in China

The Alphabet Family

Eva Montanari

PaRragon

Bath · New York · Singapore · Hong Kong · Cologne · Delhi
Melbourne · Amsterdam · Johannesburg · Shenzhen

Here is a house
with a bright red roof.
It has a funny little door
with a funny little handle.

And if you open it...

...you'll meet
Mommy A.

She wants to write a story,
but the page is blank and her head
is empty, without letters, without ideas.

But a sudden

hubbub
hullabaloo
makes her hurry downstairs...

...into the
midst of a great
orchestra...

...then into a race!
Go slowly, slowly.

Then walk, trot, canter, gallop!

Then fast, fast race until...

...you lose
your way in the dark.

There's a light!

Now find Mommy A
in the garden.

Look at the grass grow.

Breathe in the scent
of the flowers!

Chase after flying bugs...

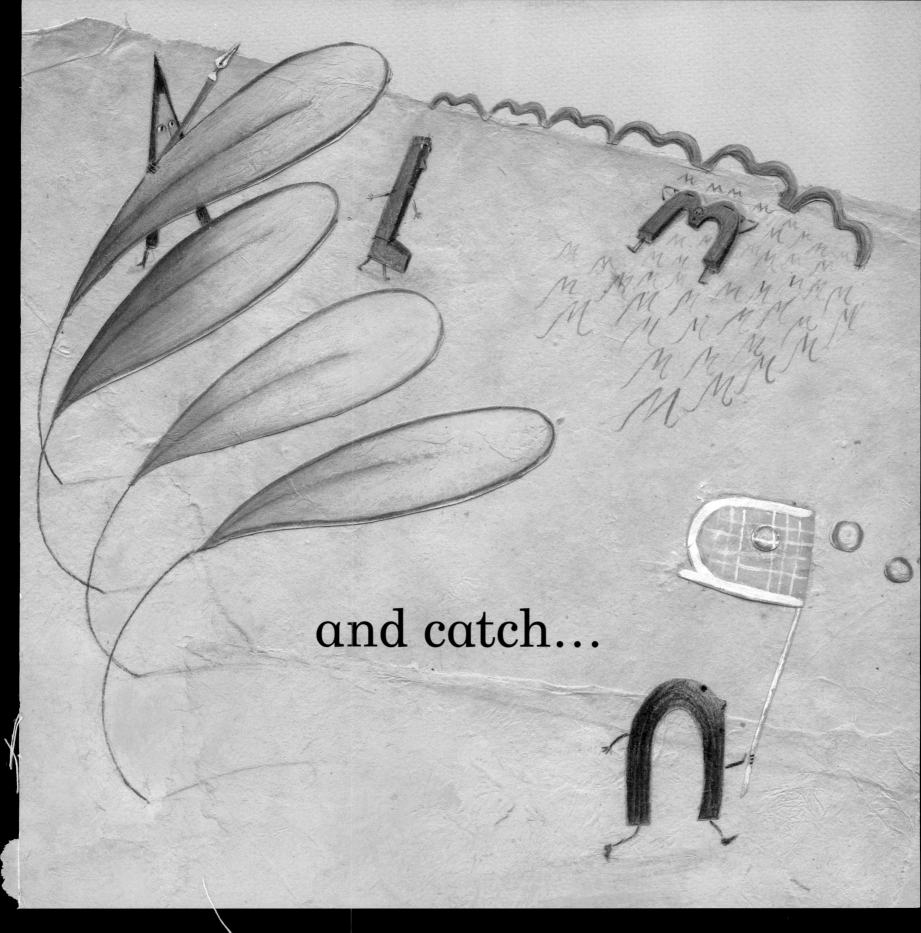

and catch...

...soap bubbles!

If you're hungry,
have some food.

There's some
of every shape
and size!

Follow Mommy A
from one room
to the next.

If you need to brush your teeth,
get in line and wait, because...

...there's always someone in the bathroom!

Now all the little letters follow Mommy A…

...into the next-to-last
room of the house.

It is time to listen to her story!

Wait in silence with all the little letters.
Mommy A is sorting out her letters
and her ideas.

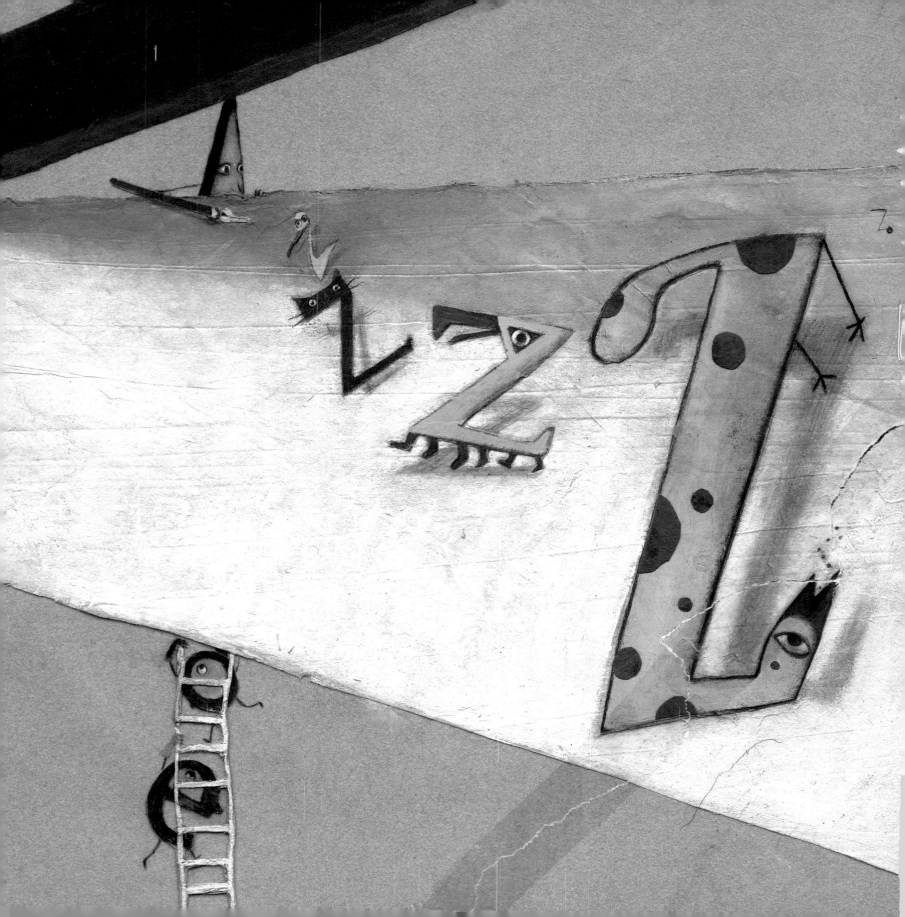

...the dreams of
Daddy Z!

Now Mommy A and little

b c d e f g h i j k l m n

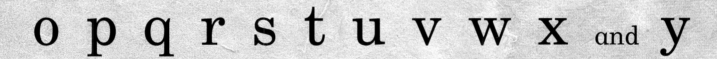

o p q r s t u v w x and y

snuggle with
Daddy Z!

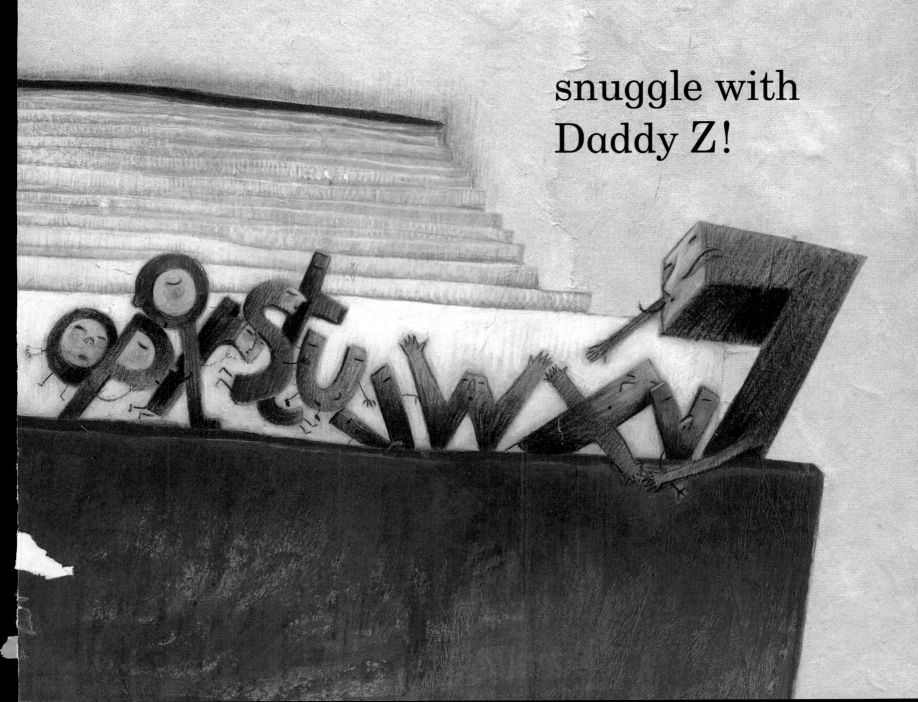

Leave the Book-House
without making
any noise.

Hush,
shhh,
gently,
silently.

Let the Alphabet
Family sleep.

Now it's **your** turn
to tell us a story.